For Gemk,

Whose endless supply of ideas and honest critique made this possible.

感謝 Gemk

源源不絕的靈感及誠懇的建議讓這一切成真。

Dragon or Dragonfly

飛龍？蜻蜓！

Coleen Reddy 著

胡苣 繪

薛慧儀 譯

三民書局

On a dark, rainy day, a duke and a duck are eating dessert.
They talk about the weather.
They do not like rainy weather.

一個陰暗的雨天裡，公爵和鴨子在吃點心。

他們談論著天氣。

他們都不喜歡下雨天。

The duck sees something on his dessert.
"Look!" says the duck. "It's a dragon."
"A DRAGON!" yells the duke.

鴨子看見他的點心上面有一樣東西。
「看哪！」鴨子說。「是一隻飛龍呀！」
「一隻飛龍！」公爵大叫了起來。

"Let's run away before it kills us," says the duck.
Dragons are dangerous and the duck is very scared.
"But are you sure that it is a dragon?"
asks the duke.

「我們快逃呀！免得這隻飛龍殺了我們！」鴨子說。
飛龍很危險，所以鴨子非常害怕。
「但你確定這真的是隻飛龍嗎？」公爵問。

They look at the little thing on the dessert.
"I don't think that it is a dragon," says the duke.
"What do you mean?" asks the duck.

他們看著點心上頭的小東西。
「我不認為牠是一隻飛龍啊。」公爵說。
「為什麼?」鴨子問。

10

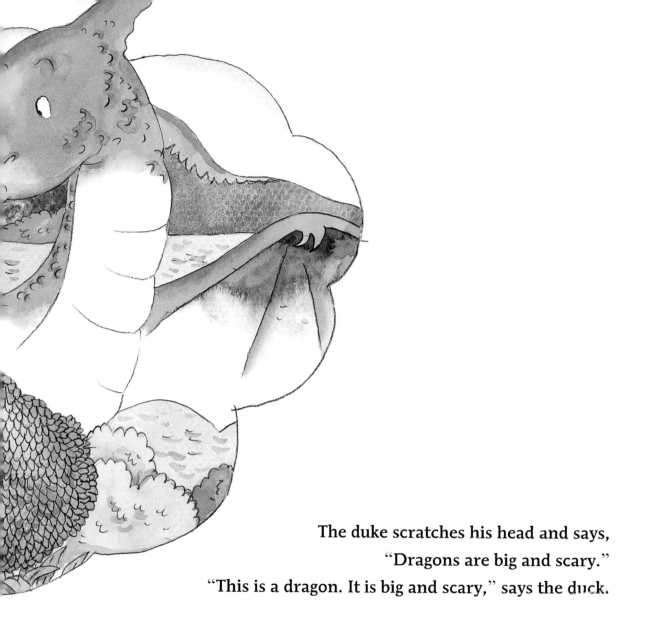

The duke scratches his head and says,
"Dragons are big and scary."
"This is a dragon. It is big and scary," says the duck.

公爵搔搔他的頭，說：「飛龍都是又大又嚇人的。」
「這就是飛龍呀！牠是又大又嚇人呀！」鴨子說。

12

"No, no, dragons are BIGGER.
Dragons are as big as dinosaurs."
"But it is still scary."
"No, no, it is so little.
We are bigger than it.
It is not scary."

「不不不，飛龍更大。飛龍和恐龍一樣大呢！」
「但是牠看起來還是很嚇人呀。」
「不不不，牠這麼小，我們比牠還要大。牠根本不可怕。」

13

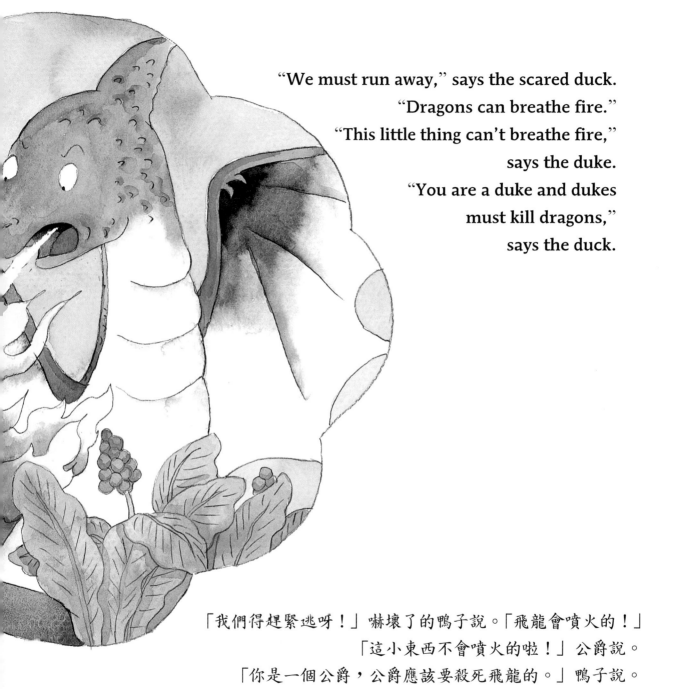

"We must run away," says the scared duck.
"Dragons can breathe fire."
"This little thing can't breathe fire,"
says the duke.
"You are a duke and dukes
must kill dragons,"
says the duck.

「我們得趕緊逃呀！」嚇壞了的鴨子說。「飛龍會噴火的！」
「這小東西不會噴火的啦！」公爵說。
「你是一個公爵，公爵應該要殺死飛龍的。」鴨子說。

"No, no, I am sure that this is not a dragon."
"But it has wings and can fly, dragons can fly, too."
"But it is too little to hurt us."

「不不不，我確定這不是一隻飛龍。」
「但是牠有翅膀，還能飛呢！飛龍也會飛呀！」
「可是牠太小了，根本傷害不了我們。」

Just then, the little thing starts to fly about the room.
"It's getting away," says the duck.
"Kill it before it gets away!"
The duke takes his sword out
and tries to kill the little thing.

就在這時，這小東西開始在房間裡頭飛來飛去。
「牠要逃走了！」鴨子喊著。「快殺了牠，免得牠跑掉呀！」
公爵拿出他的劍，想殺了這小東西。

19

"Stop, stop," cries the little thing.
"What's that? The dragon can speak,"
says the duck.
"Don't kill me."

「住手！住手！」這小東西大叫著。
「怎麼回事？這隻飛龍會說話耶！」鴨子說。
「不要殺我呀！」

"I am not a dragon."

"What are you?" asks the duke.

"I am a DRAGONFLY."

「我不是飛龍。」

「那你是什麼?」公爵問。

「我是蜻蜓。」

"What is a dragonfly?" asks the duck.

"Are you a DRAGON that can FLY?" asks the duke.

"No, I am not a dragon at all."

「蜻蜓是什麼？」鴨子問。

「你是一隻會飛的龍嗎？」公爵問。

「不，我根本不是龍啊！」

24

"I am an insect."
"Can you breathe fire or kill anything?" asks the duck.
"No, I cannot breathe fire and I do not kill anything."

「我是一隻昆蟲。」
「你會噴火或害人嗎?」鴨子問。
「不,我不會噴火,也不會害人。」

"I am sorry that I tried to kill you," says the duke.
"We thought that you were a dangerous, fire-breathing dragon," says the duck.
"I am just a little insect," says the dragonfly.

「對不起，我剛剛還想要殺了你呢！」公爵說。
「我們以為你是一隻會噴火的危險飛龍。」鴨子說。
「我只是隻小飛蟲啦！」蜻蜓說。

29

"Would you like some dessert?" asks the duke.

"Yes," says the dragonfly.

The dragonfly, the duke and the duck eat some dessert.

「你要不要來些點心?」公爵問。

「好呀!」蜻蜓說。

於是蜻蜓、公爵和鴨子便一塊兒吃起點心來了。

會扭腰的飛龍

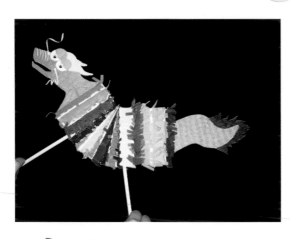

1. 西卡紙　　　　5. 雙面膠
2. 彩色筆　　　　6. 彩紋紙
3. 剪刀　　　　　7. 筷子×2
4. 刀片

＊在做勞作之前，要記得在桌上先鋪一張紙或墊板，才不會把桌面弄得髒兮兮喔！

步　驟

(1) 龍的身體

　　1. 將西卡紙割成一個長條形，折成如右圖。

　　2. 用彩紋紙在折好的長條形上做裝飾。

　　3. 將筷子固定在龍身的兩端。

(2) 龍頭與龍尾

　　1. 在西卡紙上畫上你心目中龍頭及龍尾的模樣。

　　2. 剪下畫好的龍頭及龍尾，分別用雙面膠固定在龍身的兩端。

可以用筷子控制龍扭腰擺臀的速度、節奏喔！

32

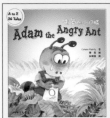

A to Z
26 Tales

二十六個妙朋友，陪你一起

愛閱雙語叢書

✿26個妙朋友系列✿

二十六個英文字母，二十六冊有趣的讀本，最適合初學英文的你！

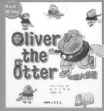

快樂學英文！

精心錄製的雙語CD，
　　讓孩子學會正確的英文發音
用心構思的故事情節，
　　讓兒童熟悉生活中常見的單字
特別設計的親子活動，
　　讓家長和小朋友一起動動手、動動腦

探索英文叢書

中高級·中英對照

波波唸翻天系列

你知道可愛的小兔子也會 "碎碎唸" 嗎？

波波就是這樣。

他將要告訴我們什麼有趣的故事呢？

波波的復活節／波波的西部冒險記／波波上課記／我愛你，波波
波波的下雪天／波波郊遊去／波波打球記／聖誕快樂，波波／波波的萬聖夜

共 9 本，每本均附 CD

國家圖書館出版品預行編目資料

Dragon or Dragonfly:飛龍？蜻蜓！ / Coleen Reddy
著;胡苕繪;薛慧儀譯.－－初版一刷.－－臺北
市；三民，2003
　　面；　公分－－(愛閱雙語叢書. 二十六個妙朋
友系列) 中英對照
ISBN 957-14-3775-1　(精裝)

1.英國語言－讀本

523.38　　　　　　　　　　　　　　92008841

© **Dragon or Dragonfly**
——飛龍？蜻蜓！

著作人　Coleen Reddy
繪　圖　胡苕
譯　者　薛慧儀
發行人　劉振強
著作財
產權人　三民書局股份有限公司
　　　　臺北市復興北路386號
發行所　三民書局股份有限公司
　　　　地址／臺北市復興北路386號
　　　　電話／(02)25006600
　　　　郵撥／0009998-5
印刷所　三民書局股份有限公司
門市部　復北店／臺北市復興北路386號
　　　　重南店／臺北市重慶南路一段61號
初版一刷　2003年7月
編　號　S 85637-1
定　價　新臺幣壹佰捌拾元整
行政院新聞局登記證局版臺業字第〇二〇〇號

ISBN　957-14-3775-1　(精裝)